The Buddy Files

THE CASE OF THE
MiSSING
FAMILY

Dori Hillestad Butler

Pictures by Jeremy Tugeau

Albert Whitman & Company
Chicago, Illinois

Library of Congress Cataloging-in-Publication Data

Butler, Dori Hillestad.
The Buddy files : the case of the missing family / by Dori Hillestad Butler ;
illustrated by Jeremy Tugeau.
p. cm.
Summary: Buddy the dog risks everything when he leaves his new family to
investigate what happened to his beloved Kayla and her father, slipping into a
van her Uncle Marty is using to empty her house in the middle of the night.
[1. Golden retriever—Fiction. 2. Dogs—Fiction. 3. Missing persons—Fiction.
4. Mystery and detective stories.] I. Tugeau, Jeremy, ill. II. Title.
III. Title: Case of the missing family.
PZ7.B9759Buf 2010
[Fic]—dc22

Published in 2010 by Albert Whitman & Company.
ISBN 978-0-8075-0912-8 (HC)
ISBN 978-0-8075-0934-0 (PB)

Printed in the United States of America
12 11 10   9   8   7   LB 20 19 18 17 16 15

The design is by Nick Tiemersma.

For more information about Albert Whitman & Company,
please visit our web site at www.albertwhitman.com.

For Kathy,
Editor Extraordinaire

Table of Contents

1
No Jumping to Conclusions

Hello!

My name is Buddy. I'm a dog, but I'm also a detective.

I used to solve mysteries with my old human, Kayla. Now I solve them by myself.

Here is a list of mysteries I've solved:

- 🐾 The Case of the Missing Boy
- 🐾 The Case of the Mixed-Up Mutts

Those were easy cases to solve. I'm working on another case that is much harder to solve. I call it the Case of the Missing Family.

I'm a pretty lucky dog. I have both an old family and a new family. The people in my new family are:

🐾 Connor 🐾 Mom

They are not missing. They're inside that house over there. It's nighttime, so they're asleep. I love my new family, but I can't help wondering what happened to my old family. My old family is the family that is missing.

The people in my old family are:

🐾 Kayla

🐾 Dad

🐾 Mom

Sometimes when my new family
is asleep, I come outside, lie down
under the stars, and gaze at my old
family's house. My old family used
to live in the house behind this one,
but they haven't been there in a long
time. There is a sign in their front

yard. It says: For Rent. That means:

- 🐾 **My old family isn't coming back to Four Lakes.**
- 🐾 **A new family will move into their house.**

I know where the mom from my old family is. She's in a place called the National Guard. She's been there for eleventy-hundred-thousand days. I don't know what happened to Kayla and Dad. That is the mystery.

If you want to solve a mystery, you should make a list of things you know and things you don't know. That will help you make a plan so you can solve the case.

Here is what I know:

- Kayla and Dad left me at Barker Bob's.
- They said they were going to visit Grandma in Springtown and that they would be back in one week.
- They never came back.
- There was a tornado in Springtown.

Here is what I don't know:

- Are Kayla and Dad at Grandma's house?
- Did the tornado hit Grandma's house?
- Are Kayla and Dad okay?

I don't have a plan for finding out the things I don't know, but I am trying to make one. Sometimes it's hard to make plans when you have a family to take care of.

"BUDDY? ARE YOU THERE?" Mouse calls. Mouse is the biggest, loudest dog on our street. He is my best friend who is not human.

"I'm here," I say.

There is one house between my house and Mouse's house. We can't see each other, but we can hear each other. We like to catch up every night after our people are asleep.

"YOU'RE QUIET TONIGHT," Mouse calls to me. "ARE YOU THINKING ABOUT YOUR OLD FAMILY AGAIN?"

Mouse thinks I think about my old family too much. He thinks I should stop worrying about my old family and pay more attention to my new family. It's hard to do that when I don't know what happened to my old family.

"I only think about my old family at night," I tell Mouse. "After my new family is asleep. I just wish I knew what happened to them. I wish I could solve this case."

"BUDDY," he says in a tired voice. "I THINK YOU KNOW WHAT HAPPENED TO THEM."

Mouse thinks Kayla and Dad are ... I can't say it. It's too bad a word to say out loud. It's too bad a word to even *think* inside my head.

Mouse thinks that Kayla and Dad are *that word* because Kayla's Uncle Marty came and took me to the P-o-U-N-D. He says Uncle Marty would not have done that unless Kayla and Dad were ... *that word.*

I know Kayla and Dad aren't ... *that word.* Here is how I know:

- 🐾 Just because a tornado went through the town where they were visiting doesn't mean they got caught in it.
- 🐾 Just because they haven't come back home and their house is for Rent doesn't mean they are ... that word.
- 🐾 If Kayla and Dad are ... that

word, someone would have told Mom and she would have come home from the National Guard. She hasn't come home so they can't be... that word.

🐾 A dog always knows if his human is... that word. You don't even have to be there. You can sense it. I'm NOT sensing it.

There could be eleventy-twelve reasons why Kayla and Dad never came back from Springtown. There could be eleventy-ten reasons why their house is For Rent. I just don't know what those other reasons are yet.

If I thought Kayla and Dad were ... *that word*, then I would be Jumping to Conclusions. Jumping to Conclusions is kind of like jumping on the couch. It can get you in a whole mess of trouble. It's also not a good way to solve a mystery.

Mouse changes the subject. "WHAT DID YOU DO TODAY, BUDDY?"

"Mom and I practiced for our test," I say.

Mom is going to be the new principal at Connor's school. That means she is going to be the alpha human there. When school starts, she wants to bring me to school with her. She wants me to be a therapy dog. That means I get to make friends with all the kids at the school. I LOVE making new friends. It's my favorite thing!

But before I can go to school with Mom, we have to take a test. It's called the Pet Partners Team Evaluation. If we pass the Pet Partners Team Evaluation, Mom and I will be a registered therapy dog team.

"WHAT DID YOU DO TO PRACTICE FOR THE TEST?" Mouse asks.

"Lots of things," I say. "Mom practiced telling me to sit, stay, and lie down. She's pretty good at that."

"WHAT ELSE?"

"We went to the dog park and practiced walking past other dogs."

"WHY DID YOU DO THAT?"

Mouse asks.

"I don't know. It's something we have to do for the test. We have to walk past other dogs without talking to them. Even if they talk to us first."

"THAT SEEMS A LITTLE RUDE," Mouse says.

I agree. Isn't the whole point of being a therapy dog to make new friends?

"DID YOU DO ANYTHING ELSE TODAY?" Mouse asks.

All of a sudden a light comes on in Kayla's house.

I hear Mouse call my name, but I can't answer. I can't take my eyes off that light. If no one is home over there, then why did a light come on?

"BUDDY?" Mouse says. Louder

this time. "WHAT'S THE MATTER?"

"There's a light on at my old house," I say. It's the light in the kitchen. The kitchen is the most important room in a house. It's where all the food is.

Another light blinks on. It's the hall light upstairs. Then one more light blinks on: the light in Kayla's room!

Now I am going a little bit crazy inside myself.

"Mouse!" I cry. "I think my people are back!"

2
Kayla's Secret Notebook

I push my way through the dark bushes that line the fence between our yard and the Deerbergs' yard next door. There's a secret tunnel back here. I dug it myself eleventy-five nights ago.

Connor and Mom don't know about this tunnel.

I jump down into the hole and claw my way under the fence. The only light comes from the moon.

Ow! My collar snags on the bottom of the fence.

I jerk and pull, and one of the tags on my collar comes loose. It drops into the hole at my feet. Uh-oh. I think this is the tag that tells humans where I live in case I get lost.

Oh, well. I don't really need that tag. I'm just going to my old house. I'm not going to get lost.

I claw the rest of the way through the tunnel and come out in the Deerbergs' yard next door. I run through the back flower bed, into the Sanchezes' backyard, and around to their front yard. My old house is right next door.

"WAIT, BUDDY!" Mouse calls. "WAIT FOR ME!"

I turn. Mouse is barreling through the Sanchezes' yard.

"What are you doing here?" I ask as he skids to a stop in front of me.

"I DON'T KNOW WHO IS IN YOUR OLD HOUSE," Mouse pants. "BUT I DON'T THINK IT'S YOUR OLD FAMILY."

"Who else would it be?" I ask. "Who else would go inside my old house in the middle of the night?"

"I DON'T KNOW," Mouse says. "BUT YOUR OLD FAMILY IS—"

"Don't say it!" I raise my paw. If I'm not going to say … *that word* out loud, then I don't want anyone else to say it, either.

Mouse frowns at me. "WELL, I DON'T THINK YOU SHOULD GO

IN YOUR OLD HOUSE ALONE," he says. "IT COULD BE DANGEROUS."

Mouse is a good friend. Even if he thinks my family is ... *that word.*

We walk next door together, our noses pressed to the ground.

"I DON'T SMELL YOUR OLD FAMILY," Mouse says. "DO YOU?"

Actually, I *do* smell them. Sort of. It's strange. It doesn't smell like they're actually here, but their scent is stronger than it was the last few times I was here.

The scent is strongest over by the street. I look up and see a strange van parked at the curb. There's a trailer hooked to the back of the van, and the trailer is piled with Kayla, Dad, and Mom's furniture. That must be why I smell them. Their scent is on their furniture.

I gaze up at my old house. The front door is standing wide open and all the windows are lit up behind the shades. I see a human moving around in Mom and Dad's room, but I can tell by the shape that it's not Mom or Dad.

"BUDDY!" Mouse yells. "DON'T GO IN THERE! YOU DON'T KNOW WHO'S IN YOUR HOUSE! YOU DON'T KNOW WHAT THEY WANT!"

That's exactly why I *have* to go in.

I take the front stairs two at a time and go inside. Mouse is on my tail.

Wow. The living room looks … different. There's no furniture. No pictures on the walls. Just a bunch of boxes stacked next to the window.

"Raina?" a voice calls from one of the upstairs bedrooms. "Are you just about done in there?"

I know that voice.

WHO IS IT? Mouse asks me with his eyes. WHO'S UP THERE?

"Uncle Marty!" I tell him.

"UNCLE MARTY?" Mouse says out loud. "HE'S THE ONE WHO—"

"Shh!" I say. "Yes, he's the one who took me to the **P-o-U-N-D**." *What is he doing in my old family's house?*

We hear someone sneeze upstairs. Then we hear another voice. A female voice.

"Did you hear that?" says the

voice. This must be Raina.

"Hear what?" Uncle Marty asks.

"It sounds like there's a dog down-stairs," Raina says.

Mouse and I freeze.

"No," Uncle Marty replies. "There's no dog in this house. Whatever you heard must be outside. Are you ready to take some more boxes out to the van?"

"Sure," Raina says. "I hope they'll all fit."

I hear footsteps above us. The footsteps are moving toward the stairs.

"Oh no. They're coming!" I tell Mouse.

We aren't going to make it to the front door without getting caught. We have to hide!

But Mouse is too big to hide any-where in here. I motion for him to follow me into the kitchen.

Things look different in here, too. The table and chairs are gone. So are the containers of flour and sugar that used to be on the counter. Even the machines that make toast and coffee are gone. All that's in here is another pile of boxes. And there aren't enough of them to hide behind.

Then I notice the basement door is ajar. I nudge it the rest of the way open.

"We can hide down here," I tell Mouse. "But *be quiet*. Don't let anyone hear your toenails on the stairs."

I tiptoe as quietly and carefully

as I can, down the wooden stairs. Mouse follows just as quietly. Just as carefully.

It's dark in the basement, but I don't mind. I'm not afraid of the dark. Neither is Mouse. Darkness doesn't bother us.

My old family used to watch TV and play games down here. But now the TV and the shelf with all the board games are gone. The only thing left is the couch I used to curl up on with Kayla.

Hey, that reminds me…when Kayla and I were working on a case, Kayla would write about it in her detective's notebook. She kept the notebook under this couch. I wonder if it's still there?

I put my nose to the floor and sniff. There's *something* under there, something that smells like Kayla. But I can't quite reach it with my nose.

I feel around under the couch and pull out a cookie. I LOVE cookies. They're my favorite food!

I gulp the whole cookie down in one bite.

Hmm. Maybe I should have shared part of that cookie with Mouse?

No. My house = my cookie.

There's something else under the couch, but I can't quite reach it. I run around behind the couch and stretch my front paw as far as I can. Got it!

"WHAT IS THAT?" Mouse whispers. Even his whisper is loud.

"Kayla's detective notebook," I say.

I pull the notebook out from under the couch.

"WHAT'S A DETECTIVE NOTEBOOK?" Mouse asks.

"It's where Kayla wrote down the things we knew and the things we didn't know about our cases."

I slide the book into a patch of moonlight that shines through the window and flip the book open with my paw. I gaze at all the funny squiggles on the page. They swirl and curve. Some have lines through them. Others end in sharp points.

"WHAT DOES IT SAY?" Mouse asks.

"I don't know," I say. Because unfortunately, I can't read.

Kayla learned to read and write at school. This is another reason I want to go to school. Maybe I'll learn to read there, too. Just like Kayla. Then one day I'll be able to read her notebook.

But right now I need to figure out what Uncle Marty is up to.

I don't hear any sounds above us. "I wonder if Uncle Marty is still here?" I whisper to Mouse.

"LET'S GO SEE," he whispers back.

I grab Kayla's notebook in my mouth and make my way to the top of the stairs. Mouse is right behind me.

The lights are still on in the kitchen so I don't think Uncle Marty and the strange woman have left. But I don't hear them moving around in the house.

I bite a better grip into Kayla's

notebook and tiptoe all the way into the kitchen. The boxes that were stacked in here when Mouse and I went downstairs are gone now.

I peer around the corner to the living room. The boxes that were in here are gone, too.

The front door is still standing wide open. Uncle Marty and Raina are carrying boxes to the van.

I feel a low growl forming in my throat. *Uncle Marty and his friend Raina are stealing my old family's stuff!*

3
Stowaway

"ARE YOU CRAZY?" Mouse asks me.

"Shh!" I say. Mouse and I are hiding behind a big bush next to Kayla's house, and I have just told him my plan.

When Uncle Marty and Raina go back inside the house, Mouse and I will find a place to hide in the back of the van. Then we'll find out where they are going with Kayla, Mom, and Dad's stuff.

"WE CAN'T HIDE IN THE BACK OF THAT VAN," Mouse says softly.

"Why not?"

"BECAUSE," Mouse says, "WE DON'T KNOW WHERE THEY'RE GOING."

"That's why we're going to hide in the van," I say.

The only problem is I don't know what to do with Kayla's notebook. I don't want to take it with me; it could get lost. And I don't want to leave it here where anyone could find it. Hey, I know. We can BURY IT! That's what I normally do with important things I don't want to lose.

"Will you help me bury Kayla's notebook?" I ask Mouse.

"WHERE?"

I look around. "How about under

this bush?" There's soft dirt between the bush and Kayla's house. It should be easy to dig a hole here. And I don't think anyone would come along and dig it back up.

Mouse and I start digging. It doesn't take long with two of us working. When the hole is deep enough, I drop the notebook in and we cover it up with dirt.

Now we just have to wait for Uncle Marty and Raina to finish loading the van and go back inside the house.

"I STILL DON'T THINK IT'S A GOOD IDEA TO HIDE IN THEIR VAN," Mouse says out loud. "WHAT IF THEY GO FAR AWAY? WHAT IF THEY LEAVE FOUR LAKES?"

"Shh," I tell Mouse again. "It's better to be inside the van than running along behind it."

"WHAT ABOUT YOUR TEST TOMORROW? WHAT IF YOU'RE NOT BACK IN TIME TO TAKE THE TEST?"

I hadn't thought about that.

Mom and I have to take that test. If we don't, then I won't be able to go to school with her. If I don't go to school with her, I won't get to make friends with all the kids. And I won't ever learn to read.

Then a new thought pops into my head. "What if Uncle Marty is taking this stuff to my old family?" I ask.

Mouse sighs. "IF YOUR OLD FAMILY WAS STILL ALIVE—"

"They *are* still alive!" I say.

Mouse talks right over me. "IF YOUR OLD FAMILY WAS STILL ALIVE, WHY WOULDN'T THEY COME AND GET THEIR STUFF? WHY WOULD THEY SEND UNCLE MARTY?"

I don't like Mouse's questions. "I DON'T KNOW!" I yell at him.

Then I feel bad for yelling. Because Mouse is my friend, and you should never yell at your friends.

You also shouldn't yell when you're trying to hide.

"Don't you think it's odd that Uncle Marty is taking my old family's stuff in the middle of the night?" I say in a friendly, but *quiet* voice. "Doesn't that seem just a *little* suspicious?"

"MAYBE A LITTLE," Mouse says softly.

"The only way to find out what Uncle Marty is up to is to hide in the back of the van," I say.

Mouse drops to his belly. "WELL," he says, "I DON'T WANT TO GET IN A VAN THAT MAY BE LEAVING FOUR LAKES."

I can't blame Mouse for that. But I have to go. I have to find out what happened to my old family.

"I understand," I tell Mouse. "This is probably something I should do by myself, anyway."

I keep my eyes on Uncle Marty and Raina. It takes them a while to pack all that stuff in the van and onto the back of the trailer. But finally the last box is loaded. I watch as Uncle

Marty and Raina tie everything to
the trailer with a big rope. Then they
head back up the front walk.

Finally!

As soon as they're in the house,
I zoom across the front lawn. Mouse
is right on my heels.

"ARE YOU SURE ABOUT THIS,
BUDDY?" Mouse asks as I skid to a
stop in front of the open van door.

There's a lot of stuff back here.
Boxes, suitcases, even the kitchen
table and chairs. But it's all my old
family's stuff. It smells just like
them.

"I'm sure," I say. I climb into the
van and crawl around the boxes and
suitcases until I come to a chair that
is wedged up against the front seat.

There's just enough room for me to hide underneath.

"GOOD LUCK," Mouse says. "I HOPE YOU FIND WHAT YOU'RE LOOKING FOR."

I hope I find what I'm looking for, too.

"Ah-choo!" Raina sneezes. "Ah-choo! Ah-choo!" She's been sneezing since we left Kayla's house.

Raina sniffs. "If I didn't know better, I'd swear there was a dog in here," she tells Uncle Marty. "I only … *ah-choo!* … sneeze like this when I'm around dogs."

I scoot a little farther under the chair.

"It must be that dog my niece had," Uncle Marty says. "His hair is probably all over their stuff. Why don't we open the windows for a little bit? See if that helps."

I hear the windows go down. All kinds of night smells fill the van. Crickets. Owls. Wet grass. Mmm. I LOVE crickets, owls, and wet grass. Night smells are my favorite smells!

"Did you...*ah-ah-choo!*...ever think about keeping Kayla's dog?" Raina asks Uncle Marty.

"Me?" Uncle Marty says. "No. I didn't want that dog."

"Why not? It sounds like he was a nice dog. And his family sure loved him."

I don't like the way Raina says

that. She makes it sound like Kayla, Dad, Mom and I are all … *that word*. And we're not. None of us are.

"I'm not a dog person," Uncle Marty says. "And even if I was, dogs aren't allowed in my apartment."

"Well, I'd have a dog if I wasn't allergic to them," Raina says. "A big one who would go for long walks with me and play fetch. *Ah-choo!*"

I think I like Raina. It's too bad she's allergic to dogs.

"So what did you do with Kayla's dog?" Raina asks.

"I...took him to the pound," Uncle Marty says.

Raina gasps. "You *what?*"

"I didn't know what else to do," Uncle Marty says. "My brother's neighbor picked the dog up from the kennel, but he and his wife travel a lot so they couldn't keep him. I didn't

know anyone else who wanted a dog.
What else could I have done?"

He could have taken me to Kayla
and Dad. They would've wanted me.
Wouldn't they?

"I don't know," Raina says, shifting
in her seat. "It just seems like you
could have tried harder to find him a
home. What if he doesn't get adopted?
You know what happens to dogs who
don't get adopted, don't you?"

I don't know what happens to dogs
who don't adopt humans. I just know
that they disappear. Forever.

"Relax. He's already been adopted,"
Uncle Marty says. "I called the pound
a couple of weeks ago to check."

This is all very interesting, but I
wish Uncle Marty and Raina would

stop talking about me and start talking about Kayla and Dad. I know what happened to me. I don't know what happened to them.

But pretty soon Uncle Marty and Raina stop talking altogether.

I put my head on my paws and listen to the owls and the crickets and the sound of the moving van. It's relaxing. In fact, it's so relaxing I am almost falling asleep. But every time I start to drift off, Raina sneezes and wakes me up.

After one especially loud sneeze, she blows her nose. It's so cool when humans do that. I wish I could blow my nose, but I don't know how.

"How much farther is it to Spring-town?" Raina asks.

My head pops up. *Springtown?* Is *that* where we're going?

"A couple of hours," Uncle Marty says. "You can take a nap if you'd like."

I don't know how long a couple of hours is, but I know I won't be taking any nap. *Kayla and Dad went to Springtown!* Maybe Uncle Marty really *is* taking my old family's stuff to them!

4
Rest Stop

We've been driving a long time. We've been driving so long that it's starting to get light outside. Is it morning now? It could be. I'm hungry. I need to stretch my legs. And I really need to go outside.

I wonder if we're close to Springtown. We should be after this amount of time. But we're still driving.

Could Kayla and Dad still be in Springtown? Why didn't they ever come home? And why didn't they send for me? Is it because of the tornado?

I've never been in a tornado, but I've seen the *Wizard of Oz*. So I know a lot about them. Here is what I know about tornados:

- 🐾 They are big, scary clouds that spin 'round and 'round.
- 🐾 They sound like trains.
- 🐾 They can pick up a house, turn it around a few times, and put it down someplace else.

In the *Wizard of Oz*, the dog, Toto, was the hero. He moved the curtain when his human was talking to that wizard. If he hadn't done that, his human would never have gotten home.

I want to be a hero like Toto. I want to go to Springtown, find my family, and help them get back home.

It feels like the van is slowing down now. Are we here? Are we *finally* here? I wish I could see out the window.

"Ready for a rest stop?" Uncle Marty asks.

Rest stop? What's a rest stop?

"*Y-y-ah-choo!*" Raina says. Then she adds: "Yes. I'd also like to get some allergy medicine. I think I have some in that bag I tossed in the back."

The van rolls to a stop, and Uncle Marty turns off the engine.

"Can you reach your bag from here?" Uncle Marty asks.

"No. I'll need to get it from the back," Raina replies.

I hear keys jingling. The front doors open and close. Then I hear the latch turn on the back door. As the back door opens, sunlight pours into the back of the van.

I squeeze myself even farther under the chair. As far as I can possibly squeeze. I close my eyes. *Please don't notice me*, I say inside my head. *Please, please, please don't notice me!*

I feel boxes and furniture shifting around behind me.

"Got it," Raina says. The back door closes, but does not latch.

I hear Uncle Marty and Raina walking away from the van. I wiggle my way out from under that chair and climb up on top of it. Now I can see out the side window.

It looks like a rest stop is a place with lots of grass and trees. I see cars, trucks and even a bus parked beside us.

There's a small building straight ahead. I watch as Uncle Marty goes in one side of the building and Raina goes in the other side.

I have a feeling we're going to be here for a while. Since the back door didn't latch, I wonder if I can get out and stretch my legs for a few minutes.

I climb over the boxes and furniture and push against the back door. It opens faster than I expect it to. But I land on my feet on the ground below.

Freedom!

First things first. I need to find a tree or the perfect swatch of grass. Sniff... sniff... sniff... a lot of dogs have been here before me. I don't like to go in exactly the same spot everyone else goes.

But I also don't like to go in a spot where nobody else has gone before, either.

Sniff... sniff... sniff... ah, here we go. The perfect spot! I lift my leg and relieve myself.

I wonder if there are any dogs in

any of those other cars or trucks? If there are, maybe they can tell me how close we are to Springtown.

I go check out the vehicles. The little car that only has one door on each side smells like Dog. Poodle, to be exact. But I don't see any poodle around.

A rusty truck in the next row smells like German shepherd. German shepherds usually know what's going on. If this German shepherd was around, he could probably tell me *exactly* how far Springtown is. But I don't see any German shepherd, either.

I'm about to go sniff the bus when I notice the back lights on Uncle Marty's trailer blink on. The

back of the van is closed up and the
van and trailer are moving forward.

*Uh-oh. Uncle Marty and Raina
are leaving without me.*

5
Don't Be Afraid
to Ask for Help

I don't think. I just RUN!

I run as fast as I can along the side of the highway. But Uncle Marty is getting farther and farther ahead of me.

A car pulls up next to me, and a lady sticks her head out the front window. "Hey, little doggy," she says as the car rolls along beside me. "You shouldn't be out here by yourself."

There's a man driving the car and a Jack Russell terrier in the backseat.

"Are you running away from someone or are you trying to catch someone?" the terrier asks me.

"Trying...to catch...someone," I pant. I've been running so hard I can hardly breathe. "That van...with the trailer...up there."

The car pulls ahead of me and stops. The lady gets out. "Come here, little doggy." She pats her thighs. "I'll help you find your owner."

I run right on past her. I don't take rides from strangers. Even if they're with a dog.

"Have you tried the Network?" the terrier calls to me.

The Network is great if you live in

a town. If you need help or you just need to get a message to another dog, all you have to do is say so. Any dog that can hear you will pass your message on to dogs who can hear them but can't hear you.

I don't think the Network is very useful out here, so I just keep running. Who, besides this Jack Russell terrier, would hear me? And even if someone else did hear me, what could they do? I've never met a dog who was strong enough to stop a moving van.

But the terrier puts out a call over the Network anyway.

"HEY!" he shouts at the top of his lungs. "DOES ANYONE SEE THAT VAN WITH THE TRAILER

UP AHEAD ON THE HIGHWAY?
I'VE GOT A GOLDEN RETRIEVER
HERE WHO REALLY NEEDS TO
CATCH THAT VAN!"

"Stop barking, Poochie," the Jack
Russell terrier's human says. "We're
trying to help this other dog."

I keep running. Just when I think
I can't run anymore, I see the lights
on the back of Uncle Marty's trailer
come on again. The van and trailer
swerve to the side of the road and
then skid to a stop.

A car ahead of Uncle Marty stops
on the other side of the road. There is
a duffel bag sitting on the pavement.
Right where Uncle Marty would have
hit it if he hadn't swerved out of the
way.

The people from the car get out and run back to get the duffel bag.

Now's my chance. I pour on the speed.

Maybe I can catch the van before it pulls back onto the highway. I run and I run and I run. But just before

I reach the trailer, the van starts moving again.
No!
I can't let them get away. I don't know what else to do except...

close my eyes and JUMP!

I don't know if I've jumped far enough until my front paws come down hard on Dad's footstool and my back paws come down on the edge of the trailer.

Yes! I am IN THE TRAILER. The wind blows my ears up off my head.

We drive past the stopped car, and I see a Rottweiler in the open back window. He nods at me. He must be the one who pushed that duffel bag out the window.

"Thanks!" I wave to him with my tail.

"No problem," he says. "Don't be afraid to ask for help, Buddy."

How did he know my name?

There's another car coming up

fast behind us. It's the car with the Jack Russell terrier. I watch as the driver pulls up even with the van and drives beside it. The lady who tried to get me to go with them waves at Uncle Marty then points at me.

Oh no!

The last thing I need is for Uncle Marty to see me back here. I quickly dive under Dad's footstool. It's a tight fit, and I can't quite squeeze my whole body under there. But at least I'm low enough that if Uncle Marty or Raina turns around they won't see me.

Mmm. The footstool smells just like Dad. Coffee and newspapers.

Next to the footstool is Mom's

living room couch, which I was never allowed on. There are two chairs on top of the couch and…sniff, sniff…the mattress from Kayla's bed is wedged between the back of the couch and the side of the trailer. It smells like books and Kayla's blanket and everything Kayla!

My stomach growls. There's all this furniture in the trailer, but no food. And it's way past breakfast time.

I wonder if Connor and Mom know that I'm gone? Probably. I had hoped to be home before they woke up.

I see a picture inside my head of Connor and Mom. They are sitting at the kitchen table, and there are plates of bacon and eggs in front of them. I LOVE bacon and eggs. They're my favorite foods!

But Connor and Mom are not eating their bacon and eggs because they are missing me so much.

I miss them, too.

I wish I could tell them that I'll be back. As soon as I find Kayla and Dad, I'll be back.

But what if Kayla and Dad need me as much as Connor and Mom do?

I never thought about that. What will I do then?

6
HELP!!!

The van is moving slower. But it's still moving. We must have gotten off the highway. Maybe *now* we're close to Springtown.

I want to crawl out from under this footstool and see where we are. But I probably shouldn't. I don't want Uncle Marty to turn around and see me.

Sniff... sniff...

I smell cornfields. And bean fields. But I also smell gasoline and big trucks and coffee and donuts. I LOVE donuts. They're my favorite food!

We drive past the donuts and the van slows even more. Finally it stops.

Are we there? (Wherever we're going?)

It's really, really hard to stay where I am. But I know I have to. At least until I know for sure where we are.

"Over here," Uncle Marty says. "Number fifteen."

Number fifteen? What's that? A house number? Is that where Grandma lives?

Sniff... sniff... I don't remember what Grandma smells like. It's been a long time since I've smelled her. But

I smell other people in the air. People I don't know.

Unfortunately, none of them is Kayla or Dad.

I hear a garage door go up.

"Wow! This is big," Raina says.

What's big?

"Big enough, anyway," Uncle Marty says. "Let's get started."

I hear something unlatch on the trailer, and then it feels like someone has stepped up into it. Two someones, actually.

I squish myself as far under the footstool as I possibly can. The ropes that were holding all the boxes and furniture down come loose around me.

"Be careful," Uncle Marty says. "That's a heavy one."

"I've got it," Raina says.

I feel the weight of the trailer shift as Uncle Marty and Raina step back to the ground. I hear their footsteps moving away.

Slowly, I creep out from under the footstool and poke my head up above the side of the trailer.

We aren't at a house at all. We're at a long building that's full of garages! The garage right next to the trailer is standing wide open. Some of Kayla, Dad, and Mom's furniture is already in there.

I watch as Uncle Marty and Raina carry boxes to the back of the garage.

Quick, while Uncle Marty and Raina aren't looking, I hop onto the footstool, put my front paws on the edge of the trailer, and leap to the ground.

I run around to the other side of the trailer and lie down. From there, I have a perfect view of Uncle Marty and Raina. I watch their feet as they move back and forth from the trailer to the garage. They're taking everything off the trailer and putting it in the garage.

I don't get it! Why are they putting all of my old people's stuff *in here*?

Mom wouldn't like this. She wouldn't like it at all. She'd worry about her furniture getting dirty.

When Uncle Marty and Raina finish taking things off the trailer, they move to the van. While they are inside the van, I hurry into the garage.

It's pretty dark in here after being outside. I sniff along the back wall behind the couch. There's mouse poop under the couch. Mom would *really* not be happy about that.

Does Mom know what Uncle Marty and Raina are doing? Is there any way to warn her?

If there is, I don't know how to do it. I don't know if the Network reaches to the National Guard. And even if it did, would a dog I don't know be able to make Mom understand such a complicated message? Mom only understands simple Dog phrases like: *You forgot to feed me, I need fresh water in my bowl, would you like to play ball,* and *I need to go outside.*

Still, it might be worth a try. Once I'm back home.

Right now I need a plan. A plan for what I'm going to do next.

I found out where Uncle Marty and Raina were going with my old people's stuff. But it wasn't to my old people. I'm not any closer to finding them than I was before I left Four Lakes. So what should I do now?

Here are some ideas:

- 🐾 Go back to Four Lakes.
- 🐾 Get back in the van and see where Uncle Marty and Raina go next.
- 🐾 See if I can find Springtown.

The idea I like best is "See if I can find Springtown." That's the best way to find out what happened to Kayla and Dad.

But I don't know where Springtown is. It must be close. Uncle Marty and Raina talked about how far away it was. But I can't read street signs, so how will I ever find it by myself?

Maybe "Get back in the van and see where Uncle Marty and Raina go next" is a better idea. Maybe *they're* going to Springtown.

Or maybe they're going back to Four Lakes. That would be okay, too. Connor and Mom must be pretty worried about me. If Uncle Marty and Raina are going back to Springtown, it would be nice to catch a ride with them.

It would take me forever to walk back.

It doesn't matter whether Uncle Marty and Raina are headed to Springtown or Four Lakes. Either way, getting back in the van is definitely the best idea.

I creep slowly out from behind the couch so Uncle Marty and Raina don't see me. But they aren't anywhere in the garage.

Uh-oh. The big garage door is going down!

Darkness.

A lock clicks into place on the outside of the garage door. I hear the van doors open and close. Then I hear the van start up and drive away.

7
Locked In

I wander around the garage, around all the boxes and furniture. I can see pretty well in the dark. Unfortunately, I don't see a way out of here.

I go to the big garage door and scratch at it. It rattles, but doesn't budge.

"Hello? Can anybody hear me?" I call.

If ever there was a good time to

use the Network, this is it.

"HELLO!" I try again. Louder this time. "I'M LOCKED IN A BUILDING THAT LOOKS LIKE A BUNCH OF GARAGES FROM THE OUTSIDE! CAN ANYONE HEAR ME? CAN ANYONE HELP?"

No answer.

Hmm. There must not be any dogs nearby. If there were, they'd answer. Dogs don't ignore calls over the Network.

I pace back and forth in front of the door. There's got to be a way out of here.

I sniff along the edge of the garage, right next to the wall. Maybe there's a loose board or a hole I can make bigger. But I don't see any loose boards or holes.

I push against the wall, but nothing happens. I scratch at the wall. I ram my shoulder against it. I even take a running start and ram my shoulder again.

All that happens is: I get a sore shoulder.

"HELLO?" I give the Network another try. You never know when a new dog might wander by. "HELLO? CAN ANYONE HEAR ME?"

Still no answer.

My shoulders slump. I could be stuck in this garage until Uncle Marty and Raina come back.

What if they *never* come back?

I climb up onto the couch that
I never used to be allowed on, turn
around a few times, then plop down
on my belly. There must be a way
out of here. I just haven't thought of
it yet.

I think...

Then I turn around and think
some more...

I lie here for eleventy-hundred
hours and think so hard it feels like
my head might explode.

All I've come up with is:

🐾 **Mom's couch isn't as comfortable as I thought it would be.**

🐾 **I am really, really hungry.**

I wonder how long a dog can live without food?

What if a dog can only live eleventy-hundred-*and-one* hours without food? Has it been eleventy-hundred-and-one hours yet? Maybe I should search for food rather than for a way out of here. There must be *something* I can eat in this garage. Even if it's just a couch cushion.

I stick my nose between the two cushions. There are a few crumbs down there. I stand up and nudge one of the cushions all the way off the couch and ... *voices!*

I hear voices. *Human* voices.

I also hear a garage door go up, but it's not this garage door. It's the one next door. Light pours in above me. Hey, I didn't notice that the walls in here don't go all the way to the ceiling. The garages are open at the top.

I climb back up onto the couch. "Hey!" I call to the people next door. "Hello! Do you hear me?"

"Did you hear that?" a female human asks. "It sounds like there's a dog in the next garage."

"YES!" I say, rising to my feet and wagging my tail. I climb up on top of the stack of boxes behind the couch. "You're right! There *is* a dog in here! And he needs help! Can you get me out of here?"

"Oh, I don't think it's coming from that garage," a male human replies. "It's probably coming from around the building."

"No," I say. "It's coming from next door to you. The dog is NEXT DOOR TO YOU!"

"Can we see the dog?" asks a child. Probably a female child, but it's hard to tell.

"No, I don't want you two to go running off," says the female human. "We're going to leave as soon as we find the camping gear."

"Aww," the kids whine.

I can't help whining a little myself. How do I make them understand that I'm right next door to them? I'm not around the building.

I gaze up at the top of that wall. I wonder if I could climb over it and into the next garage.

There's a shelf next to me. I put my front paws on the shelf to test whether or not it will hold me. I think it will. If I climb fast. I scamper up to the top of the shelf, and it only wobbles a little. But the shelf isn't very wide. Or very deep.

I can see over the wall into the other garage now. There are a lot of boxes stacked in that garage, too. And four humans. Two of them are grown-up humans and the other two are kid humans. They all have the same kind of hair. It's the color of fire.

There's also a snowmobile in that garage. I DON'T love snowmobiles. They're loud and smelly, and when they come toward me I think they want to *kill* me.

But snowmobile or not, I have to get out of here.

I slowly raise my paws to the top of the wall. The shelf wobbles even more beneath me.

One … seven … five … JUMP!

I land on a box in the other garage.

The snowmobile doesn't move. But all four humans just about jump out of their shoes. Their mouths are like big Os when they see me.

The boy human is the first to speak. "Whoa! Where did *he* come from?" he says. He's the same size as Connor and Kayla.

"He must've jumped over the wall," says the girl. She is smaller than the boy.

"I told you there was a dog over there," says the mother.

The snowmobile doesn't say anything.

"He's so cute," the girl says as she starts to run toward me.

Her father grabs her arm.

"Careful, Lydia," he warns. "We don't know if he's friendly."

"Oh, I'm friendly," I tell them. "But you better watch out for that snowmobile."

Snowmobiles are *not* friendly.

Lydia pulls away from her dad.
"He's friendly," she says. "Look, he's smiling."

Actually I'm panting. I'm really, really nervous about that snowmobile. What if it attacks me?

Lydia reaches up and pets my front paws. Mm. She smells like cheese. I LOVE cheese. It's my favorite food!

I lick her hand in case it's got some cheese on it. Too bad. It doesn't.

"See how friendly he is?" Lydia says.

Her brother comes over and pets me then, too. He's tall enough to reach my head. I don't like it when strangers pet my head.

Lydia turns to her mother. "Can we keep him?"

What? "No, you can't keep me!" I tell her before the mother can answer. "I already have a family." In fact, I have more than one family.

"Nice-looking dog like that?" the mother says. "I'm sure he's got a family."

"Does he have any tags?" the father asks. "Maybe we can find out who he belongs to."

The boy grabs the one tag that is still attached to my collar. The other tag is probably still in the hole between Connor's yard and the Deerbergs' yard.

"His tag doesn't have his name

on it," the boy says, "It just says 'This is my ID number.'"

That's the tag that talks about my microchip. The boy starts to read the number, but I pull away. *I've got to get out of here. Now!*

Unfortunately, there is a snowmobile standing between me and the open garage door.

Be brave, Buddy. Be brave, I tell myself.

I hop down from the box, go around a bunch of other boxes and ZOOM past that snowmobile.

I am outside now. And I am FREE!

I don't think the snowmobile is chasing me, but I run anyway. Down the long driveway and into a cornfield.

I've never been inside a cornfield

before. I like it in here. It smells nice. And I really like how the dirt squishes between the pads of my toes.

But I'm not going to find Uncle Marty and Raina in the middle of a cornfield. And I'm not going to find out what happened to Kayla and Dad here, either. I'm not even going

to find my way to Springtown or Four
Lakes.

So what am I doing here?

The people from the garage next
to Uncle Marty's aren't following me.
Neither is the snowmobile. Nobody is
following me.

I stop running. I think I need
another new plan.

8
Follow That Scent!

When you don't know what to do next, you should make a list of things you know and things you don't know. That will help you make a plan.

Here is what I know:

🐾 I am not in Four Lakes anymore.

🐾 It took eleventy-one-hundred hours to get here. Give or take.

🐾 Uncle Marty and Raina are gone.

🐾 They locked Kayla, Mom, and Dad's stuff in a garage.

🐾 Kayla and Dad are not here.

🐾 Kayla and Dad are not **THAT WORD.**

Here is what I don't know:

🐾 Where am I?

🐾 Where did Uncle Marty and Raina go?

🐾 Where are Kayla and Dad?

Here is my plan:
???

I had a plan before I got locked in that garage. My plan was to hide in the back of Uncle Marty's van and find out where he and Raina were going next.

Uncle Marty and Raina are long gone, but maybe I can pick up their trail. Maybe I can follow it and see where they went.

I turn around and run back through the cornfield the way I came. The leaves on the cornstalks slap against my hips as I follow my own scent.

When I come out of the cornfield, I see that the people from the garage

next to Uncle Marty's are gone, too.
There is nobody around.

I put my nose to the ground
and zigzag around the driveway. I
smell coffee and gasoline and *Yuck!*
Cigarette butts.

Uncle Marty and Raina haven't
been gone that long. I should be able
to pick up their scent.

Sniff … sniff … sniff … ah, here
it is! Wow, I can even smell Kayla,
Dad, and Mom a little bit, too. Here
is a list of everything I smell: Mom,
Dad, Kayla, their stuff, Uncle Marty,
Raina, the van, and the trailer. I
follow all those smells down the long
driveway, past all those garages and
out to the road.

Hmm. Which way do I turn? The

smells keep going in both directions.

Wait.

I sniff again. I don't smell Kayla, Dad, and Mom to the right. I only smell Uncle Marty and Raina and their van and trailer.

I do smell Kayla, Dad, and Mom to the left, though. That's the direction we came from. I probably smell them because their stuff was on the trailer when we came.

But Uncle Marty and Raina put all those boxes and furniture in that garage. The van and trailer probably don't smell much like Kayla, Dad, and Mom anymore.

Where did Uncle Marty and Raina go next if they didn't go back to Four Lakes?

There's only one way to find out.
Follow their scent!

I start walking. There's a building
up ahead. I can tell they've got eggs,
sausage, pancakes, hamburgers, and
French fries in there. I LOVE eggs,
sausage, pancakes, hamburgers, and
French fries. They're my favorite
foods!

And I am sooooo hungry. I think
about stopping at that building. Just
for a second. Just long enough to gob-
ble up some eggs or hamburgers or
whatever I can find. But finding Uncle
Marty and Raina is more important
than finding food. So I keep going.

Up one hill. Down another. I was
already hungry. Now I'm thirsty. And
tired.

But I can't stop now because I see more buildings ahead. I must be coming to a town. Could it be Springtown?

I walk past a swimming pool, but the fence around it is twisted and bent. The pool is filled with dirt, leaves, and part of a slide.

There's a BIG van parked across the street. It is the biggest, longest van I've ever seen in my life. But it looks nice because it has books painted on the side. I watch as people go inside the van and others come back out. At first I'm afraid that some of these people are going to try to catch me because I am walking without a human. But everyone seems kind of sad and tired. They don't even notice me.

What's the matter with these people?

I sniff the road. I can still smell Uncle Marty and Raina's scent. I can almost smell Kayla and Dad's scents, too. But I'm pretty sure that's just wishful smelling.

I follow Uncle Marty's scent down the street and around a corner. I pass houses that are missing roofs and part of their walls. There are Dumpsters parked in front of some of these houses. The farther I walk, the worse things look. In some places it looks like there are whole buildings and trees missing.

Is this what happens when a tornado rips through a town?

I follow Uncle Marty's scent around another corner. There are people working on this street. Some are working on street lights and utility poles. Others are working on houses. No one is talking, they're just working.

A lot of the houses have tents and campers parked on the front lawns. Are people living in tents and campers while their houses are fixed up?

I spot Uncle Marty's van and empty trailer up ahead. There's a camper in the small yard next to the van and trailer. The house behind it is missing the roof and part of the walls.

I sniff the trailer, the van, the

tiny yard in front of the camper and all of a sudden my heart stops. This isn't wishful smelling. *I smell Kayla!* Not her stuff, but *her.*

She's here!

Well, maybe she's not here right now. But she's been here. She's been here recently.

Hey, there's a book over on the tree stump. It's got a red train car at the top, and some writing, and a picture of a dog and four kids. *I know that book!* Kayla used to read it to me all the time. It's her FAVORITE book! And it has her scent all over it.

"Kayla, are you here?" I call out. My tail is going eleven-million-hundred-jillion miles an hour!

"KAYLA? CAN YOU HEAR ME? WHERE ARE YOU, KAYLA?"

I knew she wasn't...*dead*. I just knew it!

So where is she?

I sniff all around the yard. Around the camper. Around the broken house behind the camper. I smell Kayla. And Dad, too. I *know* it's them. But I don't see them.

"KAYLA!!!" I yell as loud as I can. "KAYLA, CAN YOU HEAR ME???"

The door to the camper swings open. A lady in a flowery house dress steps outside. *It's Grandma!*

Grandma and I have never been the best of friends. We had a little misunderstanding over a slipper once. But we're family, so I think we should forgive and forget.

I zoom across the yard. When I reach her, I throw myself at her. "IS KAYLA HERE? IS KAYLA HERE? IS KAYLA HERE?" I ask, trying to talk and kiss her cheek at the same time.

Grandma pushes me away. "Get away, Dog!"

It's sad that some family members don't like to be kissed by other family members.

"You do recognize me, don't you, Grandma?" I ask. I'm not sure that she does.

I kiss her hand and her leg, then turn my backside to her so she can smell me if she wants.

"I said, 'get away!'" Grandma

cries. She waves her hands at me.
"Shoo! Bad dog!"

Bad dog? What did I do?

Grandma goes back inside the
camper. She doesn't invite me in.
And she doesn't offer me anything
to eat or drink. She just watches me
from behind the screen door. "You go
away or I'll call the dogcatcher," she
warns.

The dogcatcher? I gulp.

"You don't need to call the dogcatcher," I tell Grandma. "Please,
I just want to see Kayla and Dad.
Are they in there? I know you know
where they are. Can you take me to
them?"

The inside door slams shut.

Grandma lifts the shade on the

window and peers out at me. Uh-oh.
Is that a phone in her hand? Was she
serious about calling the dogcatcher?

I'd better get out of here.

But where am I going to go?

9
Answers

I'm not leaving until I find Kayla. Her scent is all over this yard. But I don't think she's here now. If she was, she would have heard me calling for her, and she would have come outside.

I sniff for a trail to follow, but none of the trails I pick up seem to go anywhere. They just go in circles around the yard.

Maybe I should try the Network.

"Hello?" I call. "Can anyone hear me? I'm looking for my old human. I know she's in this town somewhere. Can someone help me find her?"

Nobody answers.

I heard there were dogcatchers in Springtown right after the tornado. A lot of dogs lost their homes in the tornado, so the dogcatchers came and took them to P-o-U-N-Ds in other towns. Did they take *all* the dogs away? Is that why nobody is answering me?

I may have to find Kayla on my own. But how?

I glance over at that book on the tree stump. Then I remember that big van I passed on my way into town. The one that had pictures of books on it. I wonder if that big van is some sort of library on wheels? I LOVE libraries. So does Kayla. They are our favorite thing! *Could Kayla be there?*

I pick up the book in my mouth and hurry back to where I saw that van. I have a good feeling about this. A *very* good feeling.

I round the corner... keep running down another street... turn another corner... and then I stop. That big van is right in front of me. I watch as the door opens and somebody steps outside. A girl with dark braids. My heart starts to pound. *Could it be?*

The girl sees me at almost the exact same time as I see her. Her mouth drops open. Then her whole face lights up.

"King?" she cries.

I drop the book. "Kayla!" I say.

We are running to each other as fast as we both can run.

"Is it you, King? Is it really you?" Kayla asks as she throws her arms around me.

"It's me," I tell Kayla as I kiss her all over. "It's really me. Except my name isn't King anymore. It's Buddy."

"I never thought I'd see you again," Kayla says. "How did you ever find me?"

"Well," I say. "It's kind of a long story..."

Kayla spots the book I dropped

on the grass. "And you even brought my book!" She runs to grab it. "That means you looked for me at Grandma's house first, then you came here."

"I sure did!" I wag my tail. Kayla is such a good detective!

"C'mon." She hugs me some more. Then she says, "Let's go back to Grandma's house."

"Okay," I say, trotting after her. I would follow her anywhere.

"I heard Uncle Marty said he took you to the pound," Kayla says as we turn the corner. "I was really mad when I found out. He was supposed to find you a new home, not take you to the pound."

"It's okay," I say. "I found a new

home—" *Right behind yours.*

"There was a tornado here," Kayla interrupts. "That's why Dad and I never came back. And now Dad wants to stay here and help rebuild the town. He even talked to Mom about us building a new house here so we can be closer to Grandma."

So that's why there was a sign that said For Rent in front of their house in Four Lakes.

"But I don't think we're going to get a new house anytime soon," Kayla says glumly. "Dad got hurt working on Grandma's house. He's in the hospital."

Oh no! "Is he okay?" I ask.

"He'll be okay," Kayla says. "But

I miss him and Mom and you so much!"

I lick her leg. "I've missed you, too," I tell her.

"Dad said it would be too hard to have you here when we're all working so hard," Kayla goes on. "That's why he told Uncle Marty to find you a new home. But now that you're here, he and Grandma won't send you back to Four Lakes. I know they won't! Now that you're here, you can stay forever!"

Forever? But... what about Connor and Mom?

We are back at Grandma's camper now. Kayla and I sit down together on the grass out front, and I rest my head on her knee. She runs her hand down my whole body, from my head to my tail. Just the way I like it.

"Some new people are moving into our house in Four Lakes today," Kayla says.

That's why Uncle Marty and Raina came and moved Kayla, Dad, and Mom's stuff out of the house last night. Dad couldn't do it, he's in the hospital.

And since Kayla and Dad don't have a new house yet, Uncle Marty and Raina had to put Kayla, Dad, and Mom's stuff in a big garage.

I've solved the Case of the Missing Family and answered all

my questions except this one:

🐾 **Will I stay here with Kayla or will I go back to Connor and Mom?**

I know Kayla wants me to stay here. But Connor and Mom would want me to come home.

I don't think a dog can have two families especially if those families don't live in the same town.

"Kayla!" says a sharp voice behind us. It's Grandma. She's standing at the door of the camper.

"What are you doing with that dirty dog?" Grandma asks.

Dirty dog? I just had a bath twelve or seven days ago.

Kayla brushes some dirt and cornstalk stuff off my coat. "This isn't just any old dog," she tells Grandma. "It's *King!* I don't know how he found me, but he did! Isn't it wonderful?"

Grandma shakes her head. "That's not your dog, honey," she says. "Your dog is with another family in Four Lakes. This dog just looks like your dog."

"No, this is King," Kayla says. "I know it is."

"Well, even if he was your dog," Grandma says, "you wouldn't be able to keep him. There's no room for a dog in this tiny camper."

10
Back Where I Belong

Water pools inside Kayla's eyes, then dribbles down her cheeks.

Grandma steps outside and walks over to us. "I know you miss your dog, honey," she says in a soothing voice. "But you'll get a new dog when you move into your new house. That's what your dad said."

"I don't want a new dog," Kayla cries. "I want King." She hugs me.

The door to Grandma's trailer opens again. This time Uncle Marty steps outside. "What's going on?" he asks.

"Kayla thinks this stray dog is her dog," Grandma says.

Stray dog? "I'm not a stray. I *am* her dog," I tell Grandma. I can't believe Grandma doesn't recognize me.

"That's not your dog, Kayla," Uncle Marty says. "Your dog has a nice new family. I called the pound and checked on him myself."

"He is *too* my dog," Kayla insists. "Do you think I don't know my own dog?"

Grandma and Uncle Marty talk to each other with their eyes. But I can understand what they're saying. They're saying they're tired. They're worried. And no matter what Kayla says, they don't believe I'm really her dog.

Finally, Grandma says out loud, "Why don't we call the hospital and talk to your dad, Kayla. We'll see what he has to say about all of this."

"Okay," Kayla says with a sniff. She runs to the camper and goes inside with Grandma and Uncle Marty.

I hurry after them, but the door closes before I get there.

"You stay outside." Grandma points her finger at me.

It's okay. I don't mind staying outside. I can still hear Kayla's part of the conversation.

I listen as she tells Dad about how she came out of the bookmobile and there I was! "Can you believe it?" she cries. "We can keep him, can't we? He came all this way! And he doesn't take up much room. He can sleep with me!"

I can't hear what Dad is telling her, but I can tell Kayla doesn't like it.

"Please, Daddy," she says in a small voice. Sad sounds come out of her nose and her mouth.

All of a sudden I hear the phone clatter to the floor. The camper door bursts open, and Kayla runs outside. She flings her arms around me and hugs me so tight she's squeezing the air right out of me. Water pours out of her eyes and soaks into my coat.

Dad must have told Kayla I couldn't stay.

Grandma comes outside then. She walks over to us. "We just can't take care of a dog right now," she tells Kayla, rubbing her back. "I wish we could, but we can't."

I'm not sure Grandma *really* wishes they could take care of me. But that makes me stop and think for a minute. I know what it means for a dog to take care of a human. But I never thought about what it means for a *human* to take care of a *dog*.

Dogs don't need a lot from humans, but we do need humans to feed us, give us water, and drive us to the vet when we need to go there. We also need humans to let us outside, and take us for walks, and throw the ball so we can go get it.

Wow. Taking care of a dog can be a lot of work. Especially for humans who have so many other things to worry about.

No dog ever wants to be a burden on humans.

Hmm. Maybe I should go back to Four Lakes.

I have another family there. A family that is probably very worried about me right now.

While I'm thinking about that, Uncle Marty comes back outside. "I told your dad you'd call him later," he says to Kayla. "He wants you to know how sorry he is the dog can't stay."

Kayla sniffs.

I lick her hand. "Tell him it's okay," I say. "Tell him I understand. Tell him you understand. You *do* understand, don't you? It's better for everyone if I go back to Four Lakes."

Does she believe me?

Kayla looks up at Uncle Marty. "Did you really call the pound? Do you know for sure that King has a new family?"

"Yes," Uncle Marty says. "He's with a nice family that has a boy around your age."

Kayla's eyes grow watery again. "Then they're probably pretty worried about him since they don't know where he is."

Uncle Marty presses his lips together. He *still* doesn't believe I'm King. But he pretends that he does. "Maybe we should call Animal Control so they can get him back where he belongs," he says.

"We don't have to call Animal Control," Kayla says. "If he's got a new family, he should have a tag with their name and address on it."

Well, I did have a new tag ... but I lost it when I went through the secret tunnel.

Kayla feels around my collar. "Here it is," she says, turning around my other tag. "Wait. This tag doesn't have any name or address on it."

Uncle Marty squints at the tag. "It looks like it's a microchip tag. This dog has a microchip to identify him. There's a phone number to call." He reaches into his pocket and pulls out his cell phone.

I have a feeling I'm going home.

The person Uncle Marty talked to on the phone told him to bring me to a vet. They said any vet can scan my microchip and find out who I am. Then they can call my family and tell them to come and get me.

Kayla gave me some water to drink and four or nine pieces of bread to eat. I LOVE bread. It's my favorite food!

Now I am back in Uncle Marty's

van and we are on our way to a vet's
office. This time I've got the whole
back of the van to myself. There
are no boxes or furniture back here.
Kayla is sitting in the front with
Uncle Marty. No one is talking.

When we get to the vet's office,
the vet scans my microchip. "This
dog's name is Buddy," he tells Uncle
Marty and Kayla. "His owner's name
is Sarah Keene. I have her phone
number right here. I'll call her and
let her know we have her dog."

I don't know if I'm happy or sad.
I'm happy I'm going home. But I'm
sad to leave Kayla.

Kayla's eyes grow watery again,
and she wipes the water on her arm.
"Can I say goodbye to him before we

go?" she asks Uncle Marty.

"Of course," Uncle Marty replies.

The vet smiles. "Why don't you say goodbye while I make the phone call." Then he goes into a back room.

Kayla gets down on her knees and rubs my ears. She leans in and whispers to me, "I'm going to miss you *so* much. But I'm glad you have a new family. I hope they're nice."

"They are," I tell her. My throat and chest feel choky. It's hard to say goodbye.

"Maybe I can visit you when I go back to Four Lakes to visit my friends," Kayla says.

I kiss her cheek. "I'd like that," I say. "And then I can show you where I hid your detective's notebook." But

I'm not sure she understands.

"Buddy's owner is on her way," the vet says when he comes back. "She sure was happy to hear someone found him. It sounds like he was supposed to take a test today so he can be a school therapy dog."

"A therapy dog?" Kayla says, petting me. "I bet you'd be a good therapy dog."

"I'm going to try," I say.

She gives me one more hug. "Be happy," she says. "I'm so proud of you!"

"I'm proud of you, too," I say. "You'll have another dog someday. And you'll take care of each other just like you and I took care of each other."

Kayla smiles at me. And then she is gone.

The vet puts me in a cage with some dry dog food and water and leaves me there for a long, long, long, long, long, long time. When he finally comes back, Connor and Mom are with him.

"Buddy!" Connor cries, running over to me.

The vet lets me out of the cage, and Connor and Mom hug and pet me all over. I'm happy to see them, too!

"I'm so glad we got you micro-chipped," Mom says.

"And I'm glad we found that hole in the backyard," Connor says.

I gulp. "You found that?"

Connor clips my I.D. tag to my collar. "You won't be getting out of the yard again for a very long time."

Well...not until I dig a new hole.

I missed the Pet Partners Team Evaluation while I was in Springtown yesterday. But the lady who gives the test lets Mom and me come and take it today.

It's a very strange test. First Mom and Perfume Bottle (that's the lady who gives the test) shake hands and pretend they didn't just meet each other a little while ago. Then Mom walks me around a bunch of cones. She also walks me past wheelchairs and past people using walkers. She even walks me past another dog. The dog doesn't talk to me, so I don't talk to him. I don't know if that's rude or not.

Mom drops a liver treat on the floor and tells me not to take it. Now that's definitely rude. But I don't take it. I have a feeling that I'll get a better treat later if I leave it alone.

Perfume Bottle pats me on the head, feels my paws and my ears, and lifts my tail. Then she tells Mom to make me sit, lie down, stay, and come.

Finally, the test is over.

"Congratulations," Perfume Bottle says. "You pass!"

Mom gives me a hug and tells me what a good boy I am. And then she gives me twenty or four bites of hot dog. I LOVE hot dogs. They're my favorite food!

"You know what this means, don't you, boy?" Mom asks.

"I get to go to school with you and Connor?" I say, wagging my tail.

"You get to come to school with me and Connor," Mom says.

Oh, boy! SCHOOL! I just know it will be my favorite thing!

About Dori Hillestad Butler

Dori Hillestad Butler is the author of more than thirty books for children, including picture books, chapter books, and middle grade novels. Her middle grade novels *Sliding Into Home; Trading Places with Tank Talbott; Do You Know the Monkey Man;* and *The Truth About Truman School* have been on children's choice award lists in sixteen different states. She's been a ghostwriter for several popular series, including Sweet Valley Twins and The Boxcar Children.

Her Edgar® Award–winning series, The Buddy Files, is a chapter book series about a school therapy dog who solves mysteries. Dori and her dog, Mouse, are a registered pet partner team in Coralville, Iowa, where they participate in a program that promotes reading with dogs.

She grew up in southern Minnesota and now lives in Coralville, Iowa, with her husband, son, dog, and cat.

Praise for The Buddy Files:

The Buddy Files

He's a dog. He's also a detective!

The Buddy Files

THE CASE OF THE
L🐾ST
BOY

Dori Hillestad Butler

pictures by Jeremy Tugeau

WINNER!
2011 EDGAR® AWARD
FOR BEST JUVENILE
MYSTERY

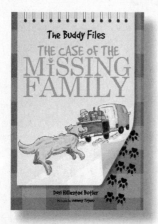

The Buddy Files
THE CASE OF THE
**MISSING
FAMILY**
Dori Hillestad Butler

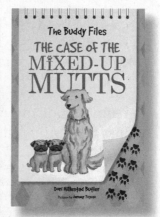

The Buddy Files
THE CASE OF THE
**MIXED-UP
MUTTS**
Dori Hillestad Butler

The Buddy Files
THE CASE OF THE
**FIRE
ALARM**
Dori Hillestad Butler

The Buddy Files
THE CASE OF THE
**LIBRARY
MONSTER**
Dori Hillestad Butler

ZAPATO POWER: THE ADVENTURES OF FREDDIE RAMOS

One day Freddie Ramos comes home from school and finds a strange box just for him. What's inside?

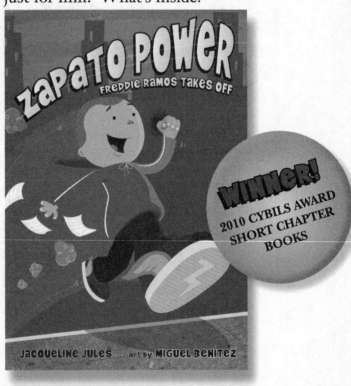

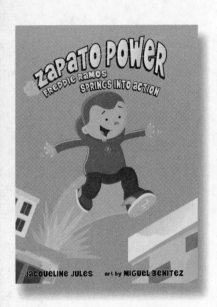

Mermaid Mysteries

There's a mystery to be solved—and the young mermaid detectives are on the case!

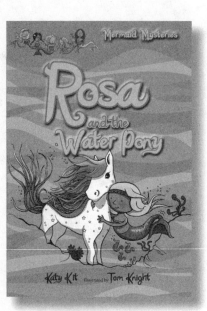

Mermaid Mysteries

Rosa and the Water Pony

Katy Kit Illustrated by Tom Knight

Mermaid Mysteries

Jasmine and the Treasure Chest

Katy Kit Illustrated by Tom Knight

Vampire School

Sink your teeth into the
Vampire School series.

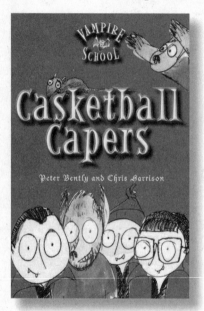

VAMPIRE SCHOOL

Stage Fright

Peter Bently and Chris Harrison

VAMPIRE SCHOOL

Teacher Screecher

Peter Bently and Chris Harrison